Got to Get to BEAR'S!

For the Snellings—the kind of friends
you can turn to in a storm

All rights reserved. For information about permission to reproduce selections from this book,
write to trade.permissions@hmhco.com or to Permissions, Houghton Mifflin Harcourt
Publishing Company, 3 Park Avenue, 19th Floor, New York, New York 10016.

hmhco.com

The illustrations in this book were done in acrylic paint on Strathmore paper.
The text type was set in Minion.
The display type was set in Blue Plaque.

Library of Congress Cataloging-in-Publication Data
Names: Lies, Brian, author.
Title: Got to get to Bear's! / by Brian Lies.
Description: Boston ; New York : Houghton Mifflin Harcourt, [2018] |
Summary: In spite of the worsening weather, Izzy the chipmunk sets off to
Bear's den in response to an urgent request from a friend in need.
Identifiers: LCCN 2016042893 | ISBN 9780544948822 (hardcover)
Subjects: | CYAC: Blizzards—Fiction. | Friendship—Fiction. |
Forest animals—Fiction.
Classification: LCC PZ7.L618 Go 2018 | DDC [E]—dc23
LC record available at https://lccn.loc.gov/2016042893

Manufactured in China
SCP 10 9 8 7 6 5 4 3 2 1
4500720315

Got to Get to Bear's!

HOUGHTON MIFFLIN HARCOURT
Boston   New York

WRITTEN AND ILLUSTRATED BY
BRIAN LIES

When Izzy read the note, she knew she had to go.

She didn't like the look of the sky. But Bear never asked
for anything, so Izzy knew it had to be important.

As she started out,
flakes began
to flutter down.

The snow piled deeper

and deeper

and deeper . . .

. . . and soon she couldn't go any farther.

"Hey!" Scritch said. "Where you headed?"

"I'm trying to get to Bear's place," Izzy said. "She asked me to come as soon as I could. But I don't think I can make it!"

Scritch nodded. "It looks a little deep. But, you know how it is—if Bear asks, you *gotta* go. Jump on my back—we'll be there in a jiff! The treetop road is the way."

So the two went on together . . .

. . . until they couldn't anymore.

Bingle landed nearby, laughing. "Slippery, innit? Where ya going?"

"We're trying to get to Bear's," Scritch said. "She asked Izzy to come."

Bingle nodded. "You don't say 'no' to Bear! But skyway is better than battling branches! All aboard—I'll get you there!"

As they went, the sky darkened, the wind grew wild, and snow stung their faces like tiny bees. "Can't see!" Bingle screeched. "Can't see!"

They came to a sudden stop.

"Maybe walking is better?" Bingle suggested.

"Maybe so," Scritch said.

"Good idea," Izzy agreed.

But it was slow going.

Snaffie caught up with them. "Hey there, everybody!" she called. "I've been following your trail. Having trouble?"

"I've got to get to Bear's," Izzy explained.

Bingle added, "But trees are bad, skyway is bad, and snow's too deep to waddle!"

Snaffie smiled. "Bear's isn't far from where I'm going—let me give you a ride!"

As Snaffie tried to jump over the snow, they sang to keep their spirits up.

"No matter how steep or tough the climb, a friend is worth it, every time!"

"Jumping's too hard," Snaffie panted. "I'm just going to plow my way under the snow. Bingle, you steer!" It worked for a while.

But as the snow deepened, Scritch
had to call out directions.

And then it was just Izzy above
the surface, pointing the way.

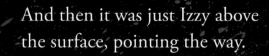

At last, the glow of Bear's place shone through the dark.

"We made it!" Izzy cried. "I hope we're not too late!"

"My f-f-feathers are frozen!" Bingle said.

Izzy knocked on Bear's door—*Tok! Tok! Tok!*—with her tiny knuckles.

Bear opened the door with the saddest look spread across her face. "Oh, it's you, Izzy," Bear sighed. "What are you doing here?"

"But you sent me that note," Izzy said, puzzled. "You asked for me."

"Yes, but I didn't think you'd make it, with this snow. Look how deep it is!"

"Am I too late to help?" Izzy asked.

"Ah, the storm ruined everything." Bear shook her head. "But you'd better come in and warm up. It's too bad—I wanted Scritch, Bingle, and Snaffie here, too."

"But they *are* here!" Izzy exclaimed. "I'm standing on them!"

Bear stepped aside as they tumbled
into the warmth of her den.

She pushed the door shut.

"So, what's wrong?" Izzy asked. "How can we help?"

Bear cleared her throat. "Well, it's not that something's wrong."

A smile crept up the corners of her mouth. She started to chuckle. "We have something to say to you."

Izzy was confused. "To me?" Her brow wrinkled.

Bear nodded. "We wanted to say—"

"How did you know it was my birthday?" Izzy asked.
     "We're your friends," they laughed. "We *knew*."
     They ate cake and told stories all through the long
night as the storm raged outside.

And in the morning, as Bear helped everyone
back home again, they all sang:

*"No matter how steep or tough the climb,
a friend is worth it, every time!"*